To my cousin Simon   AT

For Ann   DM

VIKING
Published by the Penguin Group
Viking Penguin, a division of Penguin Books USA Inc.,
40 West 23rd Street, New York, New York 10010, U.S.A.
Penguin Books Australia Ltd, Ringwood, Victoria, Australia
Penguin Books Canada Ltd, 2801 John Street, Markham, Ontario, Canada L3R 1B4
Penguin Books (N.Z.) Ltd, 182-190 Wairau Road, Auckland 10, New Zealand

Published in 1990 by Viking Penguin, a division of Penguin Books USA Inc.

1   3   5   7   9   10   8   6   4   2

First published in Great Britain by Aurum Books for Children, 1990

Text copyright © Ann Turnbull, 1990

Illustrations copyright © David McTaggart, 1990

All rights reserved

ISBN 0-670-83359-2

Library of Congress catalog card number: 89-51923

Printed in Italy by LEGO

Make It, Break It

by Ann Turnbull

illustrated by David McTaggart

Viking

AT THE BEACH

Make a sandcastle.
Make it big.

Scoop and shovel and pile up sand —
Pat it smooth with the palm of your hand.

Build the castle,
Build it high.
Build the towers up to the sky.

Now our castle is finished.
Let's jump on it!

AT HOME

Clean the bedroom.
Make it neat.

Pick up blocks, crayons, puzzles —
All the toys are in a muddle!

Pick them up and put them away:
Books on the bookshelf, pens in the drawer —
Don't leave marbles all over the floor!

Now our room is clean.
Let's play in it!

IN THE KITCHEN

Make a cake.
Make it yummy.

How much flour? Measure with care.
Watch the scales tilt — stop right there!

Crack the eggs: plop in the bowl.
Mix them in and stir it all.

Into the oven: when it's firm and brown
Take it out and let it cool down.

Now our cake is ready.
Let's eat it!